To Oscar

From.........................

Written by Katherine Sully
Illustrated by Julia Seal
Designed by Nicola Moore

First published by HOMETOWN WORLD in 2017
Hometown World Ltd
7 Northumberland Buildings
Bath
BA1 2JB

www.hometownworld.co.uk

Follow us @hometownworldbooks

ISBN 978-1-78553-586-4
All rights reserved
Printed in Italy
HTW_PO201701

Oscar
Santa's Secret
Elf

Hometown World

It was Christmas Eve and Oscar
was tucked up in bed at home.
He was trying so hard to be asleep.
But he could hear strange noises.

It wasn't the sound of sleigh bells.
It wasn't the sound of reindeer hoofs on the roof.
It wasn't even the sound of Santa unpacking his sack.

It was more of a

HARUMPH!

and an

OOF!

It was no good.

There'd be no sleep for Oscar
until he'd found out what
was making that noise.

Oscar crept down the stairs
and peered into the living room.
There were three stockings
hanging from the chimney.

One of them belonged to Oscar.
But where did the other two come from?
Suddenly, a muffled voice came from the chimney.

"Oh dear.
I'm even
more
stuck now!"

There was a scuffling sound
from behind the Christmas
tree and Oscar
jumped as a small elf appeared.

"Er, hello," said the elf. "I guess you've caught us out!"

Oscar listened as the elf explained
how Santa was stuck in the chimney.
The elf had tried to pull him out. But the only
things that had come down so far were
Santa's boots and trousers!

"I can help you," suggested Oscar.
"I'll hold Santa's feet and we can both pull."
The elf agreed. "Between us, we might be
able to get him unstuck."

Oscar grasped both of Santa's feet firmly.
But, just at that moment, a light went on upstairs.
"Oscar, is that you?" called his mum.
"Back to bed now, please, or Santa won't come!"

At that exact moment,
Santa shot back up the
chimney...with
Oscar still hanging
onto his feet.

The poor elf could not believe his eyes.
But there was no time to think...
Oscar's mum was coming
out of her bedroom.

"Just coming!" squeaked the elf.
The elf hurried up the stairs and jumped into Oscar's
bed, pulling the covers up over his head.
"Night-night, sweetie!" said Oscar's
mum through the doorway.

Meanwhile, up on the roof, Santa and Oscar
had landed in a heap. The clever reindeer had
hooked their reins under Santa's arms and
pulled as hard as they could.

"Well done, chaps!" said Santa brushing
himself down. "No more mince pies for
me tonight!"

Oscar scrambled to his feet. But Santa was so busy, he didn't notice that Oscar and the elf had swapped places!

"I think we'd better deliver the rest of the presents first," said Santa, "and leave this house till last."

Santa climbed into the driving seat.

"Elf, you get the parcels ready
for our next destination,"
he called over his shoulder.
"But I'm not Elf…"
replied Oscar.

Santa wasn't really listening.
He was talking to the reindeer.
"Up, up and away!" Santa called and
the reindeer took off before Oscar
had time to explain.

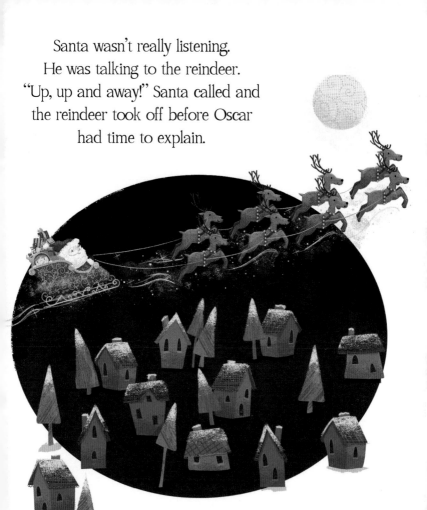

Oscar clung on tight as the
sleigh climbed high into the
night sky above the rooftops.

Surrounded by parcels, Oscar
was so busy working out which sacks were
which, there was no time to let Santa
know that there'd been a mistake.

There were big
parcels for the cities,

and SHINY parcels
for the towns.

There were ODD-shaped
parcels for the villages,

and mystery
parcels for the farms.

To: Oscar

As they landed at their next stop,
Santa decided that he couldn't risk
getting stuck in a chimney again.

"Elf, I think you'd better make the deliveries
from now on," decided Santa,
"while I sort out the parcels."

Oscar *shimmied* down chimneys.

He **Squeezed** through cat flaps.

And, if all else failed, he used Santa's *magic* key to let himself in.

In each house, Oscar collected the mince pies to take home to Mrs Santa, and carrots for the reindeer.

Finally, there was just one sack left, and
Santa still hadn't realised his mistake!
The sleigh headed back over the
rooftops to Oscar's house.

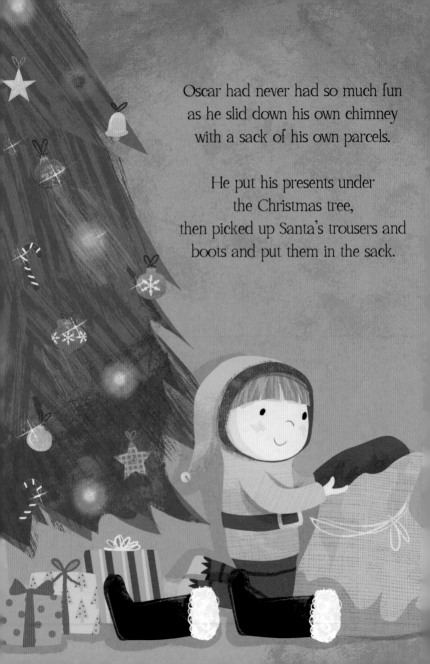

Oscar had never had so much fun
as he slid down his own chimney
with a sack of his own parcels.

He put his presents under
the Christmas tree,
then picked up Santa's trousers and
boots and put them in the sack.

"Psst! Elf, where are you?" whispered Oscar.

A very happy Elf appeared rubbing his eyes.
"I've had such a lovely sleep," he said.
Oscar handed over the sack and
waved as Elf disappeared
up the chimney.

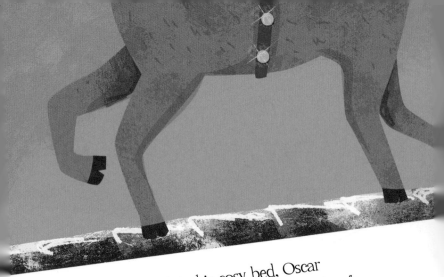

Back in his cosy bed, Oscar
listened to the sound of reindeer hoofs
on the roof, sleigh bells and, very faintly,

"Ho ho ho!
Merry Christmas!"

Or was that,

"Ho ho ho!

yummy mince pies!"?

Write your name on the parcel labels.